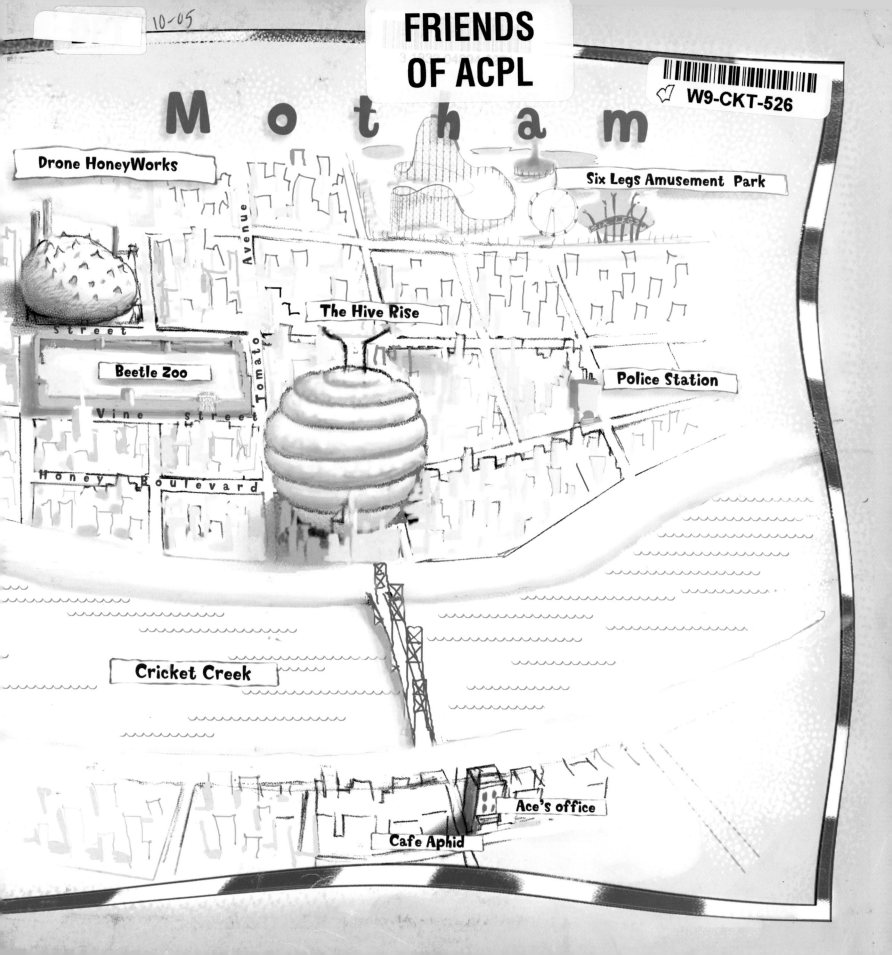

Motham

Drone HoneyWorks

Six Legs Amusement Park

Avenue

The Hive Rise

Street

Beetle Zoo

Tomato

Police Station

Vine Street

Honey Boulevard

Cricket Creek

Ace's office

Cafe Aphid

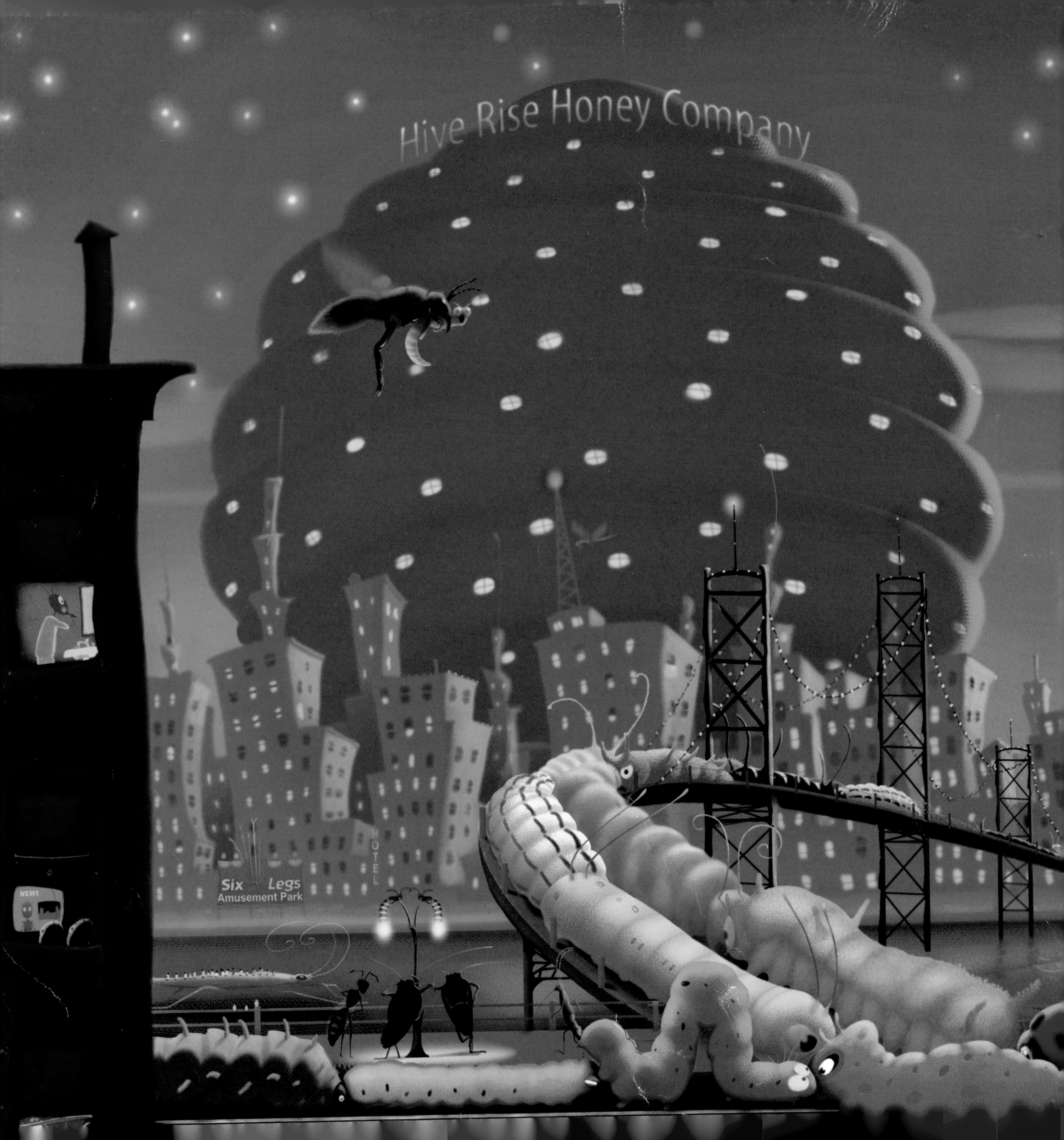
Hive Rise Honey Company
HOTEL
Six Legs
Amusement Park
NEWS

Ace Lacewing

Bug Detective

David Biedrzycki

BUZZ Radio
More Buzz Less Chirp

BLOCKBUGSTER

got milkweed?

Witchetty's
Grubs done right!

Charlesbridge

It was a night like any other night in the city. Hot and sticky. Great weather if you're a bug. Everyone's a bug in Motham City. Some good, some bad.

Bad bugs are my business.

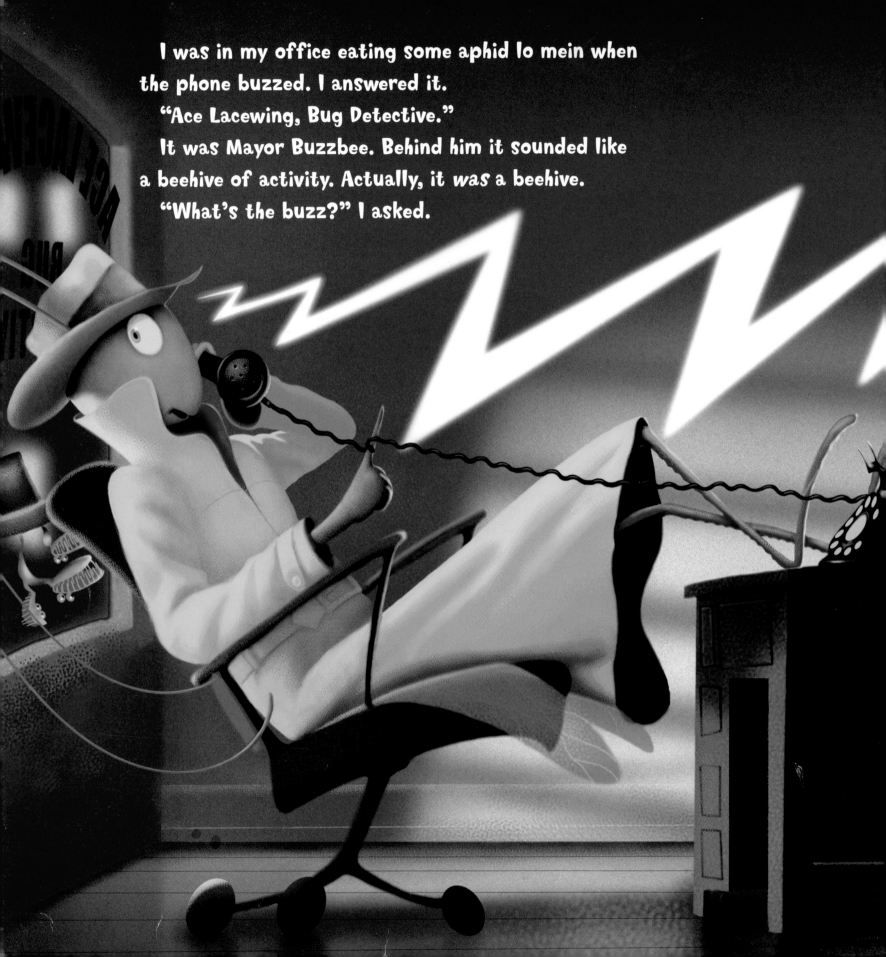

I was in my office eating some aphid lo mein when the phone buzzed. I answered it.

"Ace Lacewing, Bug Detective."

It was Mayor Buzzbee. Behind him it sounded like a beehive of activity. Actually, it *was* a beehive.

"What's the buzz?" I asked.

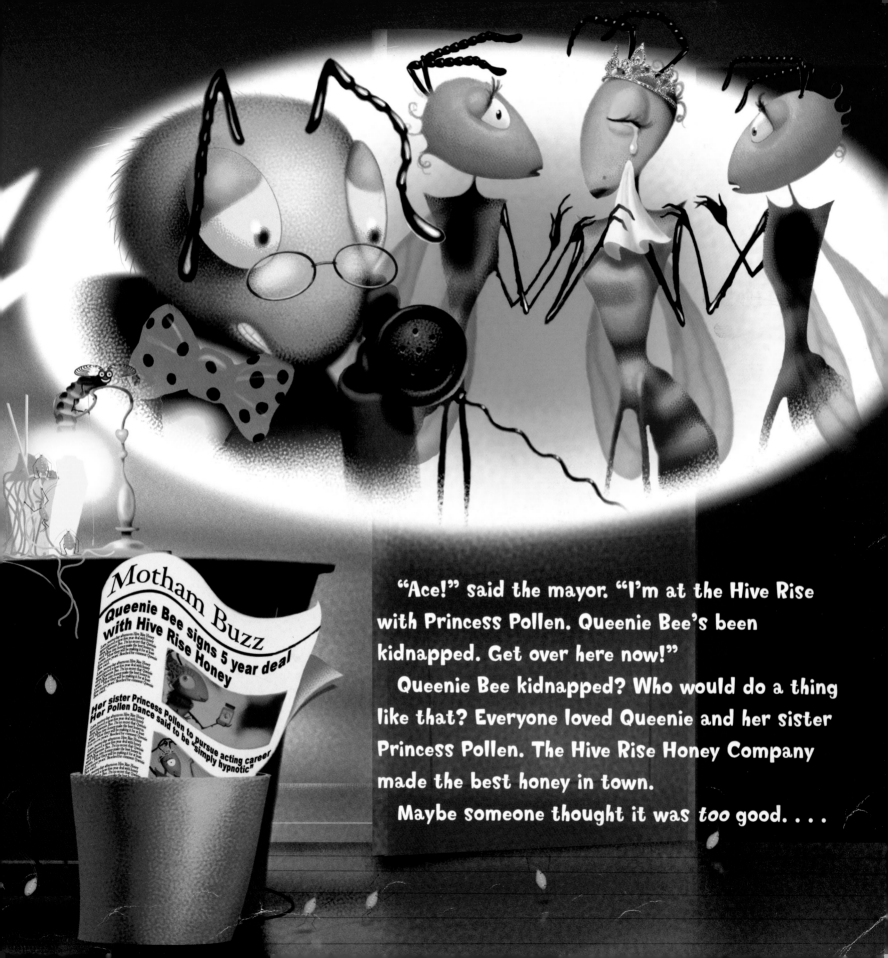

Motham Buzz

Queenie Bee signs 5 year deal with Hive Rise Honey

Her sister Princess Pollen to pursue acting career. Her Pollen Dance said to be "simply hypnotic"

"Ace!" said the mayor. "I'm at the Hive Rise with Princess Pollen. Queenie Bee's been kidnapped. Get over here now!"

Queenie Bee kidnapped? Who would do a thing like that? Everyone loved Queenie and her sister Princess Pollen. The Hive Rise Honey Company made the best honey in town.

Maybe someone thought it was *too* good. . . .

I was just about to fly out the door when I saw her standing there, like a moth drawn to a flame. Actually I *was* her flame. But she was no moth. She was the lovely rare butterfly, Xerces Blue. Doctor Xerces Blue. Not the kind of doctor who takes your tonsils out. The kind of doctor who studies bugs—dead bugs.

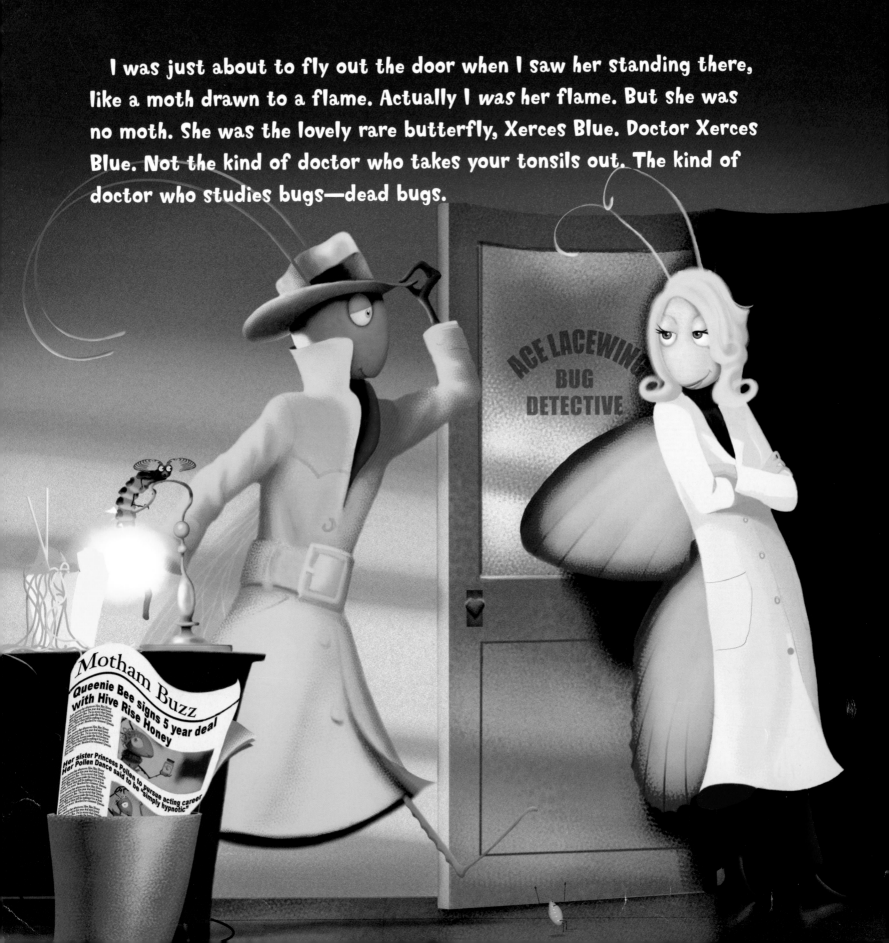

"No time now," I said. "The mayor needs my help." But those eyes weren't taking no for an answer.

"Oh, Acie," she said. "How about dinner at my place tonight? Just you and me. I'm making your favorite—aphids à la mode." How could I resist? Aphids have been my favorite ever since I was a little larva. But I also liked honey. Which reminded me . . .

"The aphids will have to stew, sweetheart," I said. "Queenie Bee's in a honey of a jam."

Downtown the traffic was crawling. That's what traffic
does in Motham. It really crawls.

"Hey, Ace!" It was Sergeant Zito, a mosquito. And a cop.
I've known him ever since we were pupae at the same school.

"Whadda ya know, Zito?" I asked.

"We have a couple of witnesses, Ace. But none of them are talking except this little maggot."

"I saw the whole thing!" cried the maggot. "I was crawling around minding my own business when all of a sudden I heard all this screamin'. I thought maybe it was a damselfly in distress. But then I looked up and I saw 'em right outside the Hive Rise—a couple of hooded bugs running off with Queenie Bee!"

"Ace?" Zito leaned over and whispered. "You believe this maggot? How could he have seen anything? He doesn't have any eyes."
I frowned.

"Which way did they go?"

"Whadda I look like, a tour guide?" squirmed
the maggot.

I should have known better than to ask directions
from a bug with no arms or legs. I told Zito to start
rounding up suspects. I looked around . . . and
noticed a suspicious trail of honey leading away from
the crime scene. I followed it.

At the corner of Tomato and Vine, I stopped in my tracks. The honey trail led to the Beetle Zoo. Lacewings have lost their heads to beetles. But I was on a case, and there was a plate of hot aphids waiting for me at the end of it. The trail went through the broken gate, and so did I.

BEETLE ZOO

SLOW
LARVAE

Have you
seen
this bug?

call
1-800
LOST

TICKETS
CLOSED

Admission
Larva..........Free
Pupa.............$6
Adults..........$10

La Cucaracha's
Restaurante
Corner of Tomato and Vine
Roaches Welcome

Skunk Beetles
Rhinoceros Beetle
Kangaroo Beetles
Zebra Beetles
Elephant Beetle
Tiger Beetles
Giraffe Beetle

Nest
For Rent

A great bug
for a great
town!

NOW PLAYING
At the
Colony Club

Ain't Miss Beehavin'

Starring
Princess
Pollen

RE-ELECT
MAYOR
BUZZBE

The honey led past the giraffe weevils. It was Hive Rise Honey, all right. Still warm.

I heard a noise, stood up, and froze!

Please don't feed the beetles!

Rhinoceros
Beetle
Oryctes nasicornis

Someone had let the tiger beetle out of his cage,
and this guy didn't want to play! He wanted to eat.
I did the only thing a bug detective worth his wings
would do. I screamed and ran . . .

. . . **smack** into a wall.
I heard a familiar flutter of
wings, and then the world
went to sleep.

Giraffe Beetle
Tachelophorus giraffa

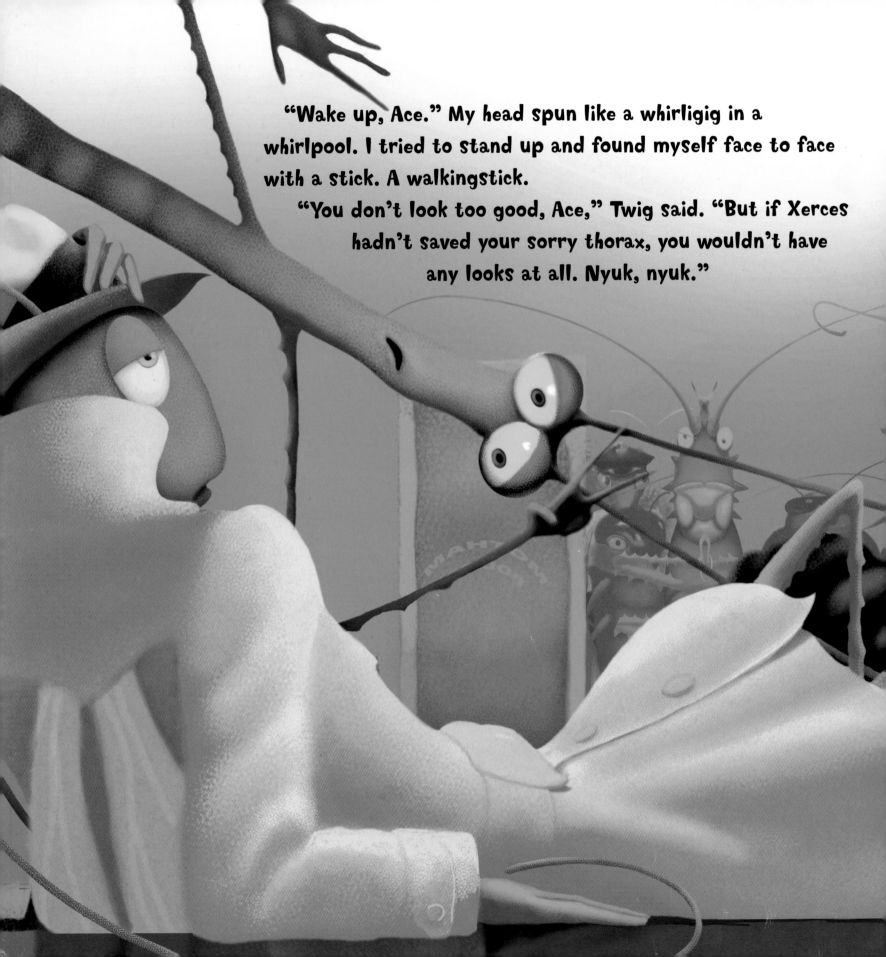

"Wake up, Ace." My head spun like a whirligig in a whirlpool. I tried to stand up and found myself face to face with a stick. A walkingstick.

"You don't look too good, Ace," Twig said. "But if Xerces hadn't saved your sorry thorax, you wouldn't have any looks at all. Nyuk, nyuk."

"Acie!!" said Xerces. "That was a nasty hit you took."

"Ahhh, it could have been worse," I groaned. "It could have been a windshield on the interstate."

I was lying in a corner of the police station. Behind Sergeant Zito, Xerces, and the maggot, a bunch of handcuffed roaches and other pests were waiting to be questioned.

Everyone had an alibi. The roaches said of course they ran from the scene of the crime—it was their nature to scatter when the lights go on. "Why do you think we wear sunglasses?" they asked.

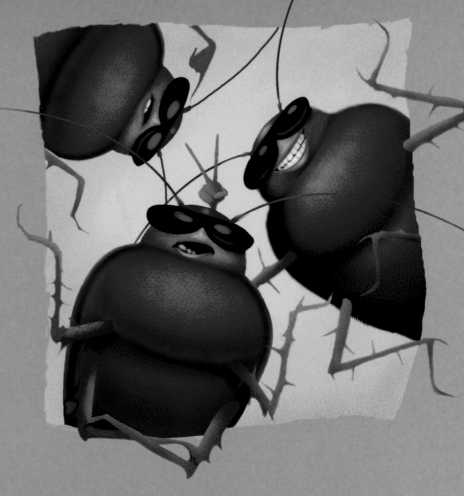

Before we could question the cicada, he molted and flew out the window.

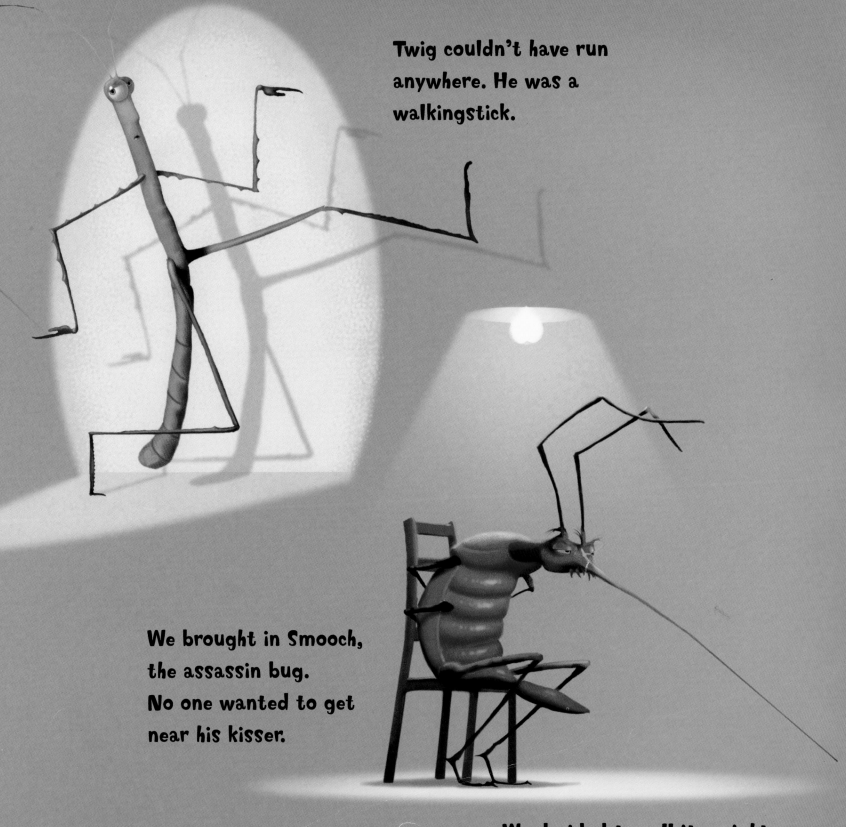

Twig couldn't have run anywhere. He was a walkingstick.

We brought in Smooch, the assassin bug. No one wanted to get near his kisser.

We decided to call it a night.

The full moon hung in the sky like a large compound eye as we left the police station.

"Psssssssst! Hey, Lacewing," a voice whispered from the shadows. "I know who's got Queenie and why."

"Who are you?" I asked.

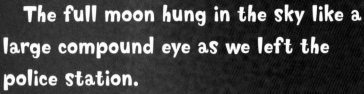

"A drone who knows the truth," he whispered. "But there are too many eyes and too many antennae around here. Let's go someplace we can talk in private."

We never got the chance.

It happened quick as a cricket—
a drive-by gassing. "Hit the dirt!!" I shouted,
but it was too late for the bee.

I couldn't make out the driver but the other one was no doubt a bombardier beetle. I could tell by the smell. I wondered if he had a license to pass gas.

I checked the bee. He wasn't moving, but he was trying to say something. I lowered my ear to his mouth.

"Drone HoneyWorks," he moaned, and then no more.

"Al the Drone," I muttered to myself.

"Al the Drone?" said Zito. "Oh no, not Al the Drone! Please don't let it be Al the Drone. Anybody but Al the Drone . . . Ace?"

"Yeah?"

"Who's Al the Drone?"

"Al the Drone owns Drone HoneyWorks," I said. "Some bugs say he has his sticky little mandibles in more than just honey. I think we should pay Mr. Drone a visit."

Xerces worked on the bee as Zito and I took off across town.

Outside Drone HoneyWorks, the smell of honey hung thicker in the air than ants on a popsicle stick. Savage mantises kept guard. As we crawled around the back of the building, I got a sick feeling in my gut. The back gate of the Beetle Zoo was right across the street. And the trail of honey led from the zoo to the HoneyWorks!

We needed a way in. But how?

Two dung beetles were making their way up the street, rolling their dung ball and collecting trash. They rolled up next to us.

"You thinkin' what I'm thinkin'?" I whispered to Zito. The dung beetles were too busy to notice us.

"Oh no, Ace, not the dung," said Zito.

"Hold your breath," I said as we leapt onto the dung ball. We rolled right past a mantis into the HoneyWorks.

I peered in a window. What I saw made my antennae quiver. In the shadows I saw someone tied up and blindfolded. It looked like Queenie. She sure wasn't getting the royal treatment here.

"Uh . . . Ace?" said Zito. "We got company." One of the mantises had followed our dung prints. He didn't look too happy. Neither were we when he tied us up and carried us inside.

Inside, the aroma of honey and pollen was sickeningly sweet. I've been in hives before. You can tell a good hive by the buzz of the bees. The buzz in here was not good. The mantis looked as if he were in a trance as he toted us past rows and rows of honeycomb.

Standing in the shadows was Al the Drone.

"Hey, boss," croaked the mantis. "Look what I found snoopin' around outside."

"Well, well, if it ain't the little lacewing and his blood-sucking friend," said the Drone.

"That's a common misconception! Actually it's the female who—uhh!" Zito groaned as the mantis's claw tightened around him.

"I know you got Queenie here, Drone," I finally squeaked. My eyes ran from all the pollen. "You'll never get away with it!"

"Funny," said the Drone, "that's the same thing Queenie said to me, and look where she is now."

He pointed behind him.

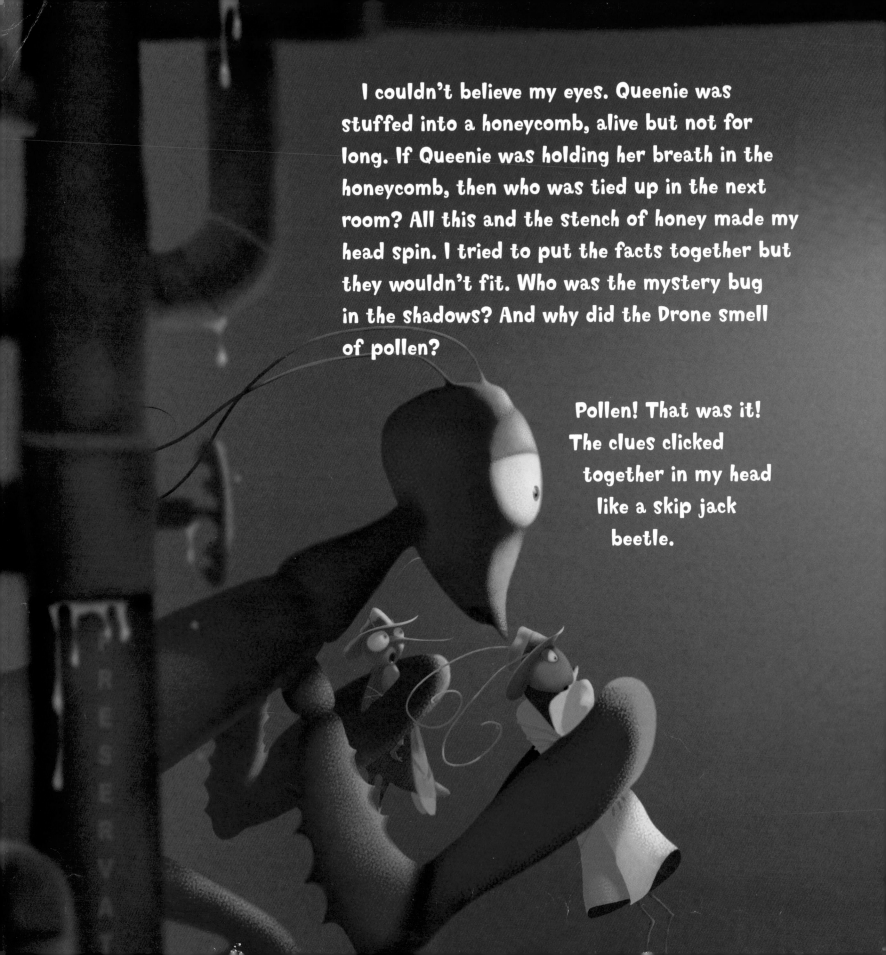

I couldn't believe my eyes. Queenie was stuffed into a honeycomb, alive but not for long. If Queenie was holding her breath in the honeycomb, then who was tied up in the next room? All this and the stench of honey made my head spin. I tried to put the facts together but they wouldn't fit. Who was the mystery bug in the shadows? And why did the Drone smell of pollen?

Pollen! That was it! The clues clicked together in my head like a skip jack beetle.

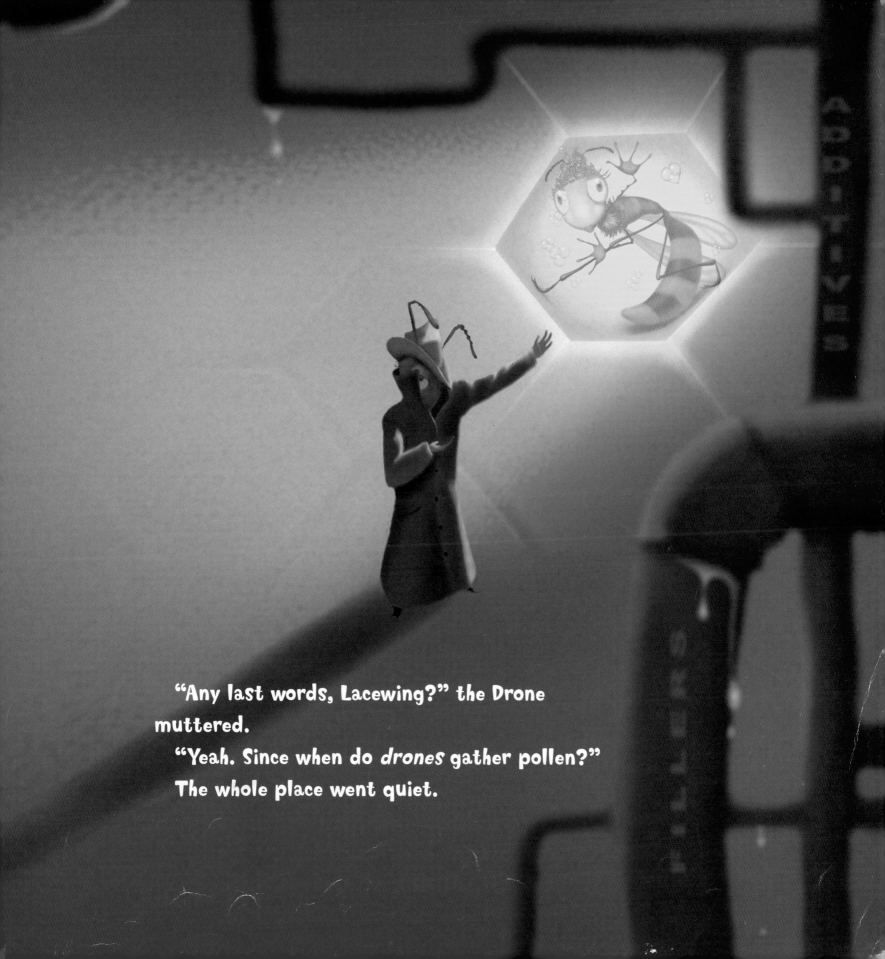

"Any last words, Lacewing?" the Drone muttered.

"Yeah. Since when do *drones* gather pollen?"

The whole place went quiet.

"Ha, you're clever, Lacewing. Clever, clever, clever," said the Drone emerging from the shadows, tossing hat and coat aside.

"P-p-princess P-pollen?!" Zito stuttered.
"In the exoskeleton," she announced triumphantly.

"But why?" I asked.

"Because I'm sick of just being princess!! I want to be QUEEN!" She stomped, mad as a hornet. "It's always Queenie Bee this and Queenie Bee that. I'll never have my own hive with her around. So I'm making it look like sleazy Al the Drone got rid of her. You guessed it, Lacewing—that's him tied up in the back room. With Queenie and Drone HoneyWorks gone, I'll be queen of the town.

"As for the mantises, they won't remember a thing. I hypnotized them with my pollen dance. You're in a rather sticky situation, Lacewing, so see ya, wouldn't wanna *bee* ya!"

Princess Pollen made her way to the door. She signaled the mantises to seal us in the honeycombs. I had to think fast. Something fluttered overhead, so I shouted the only thing that makes a mantis run for cover.

"BAT!"

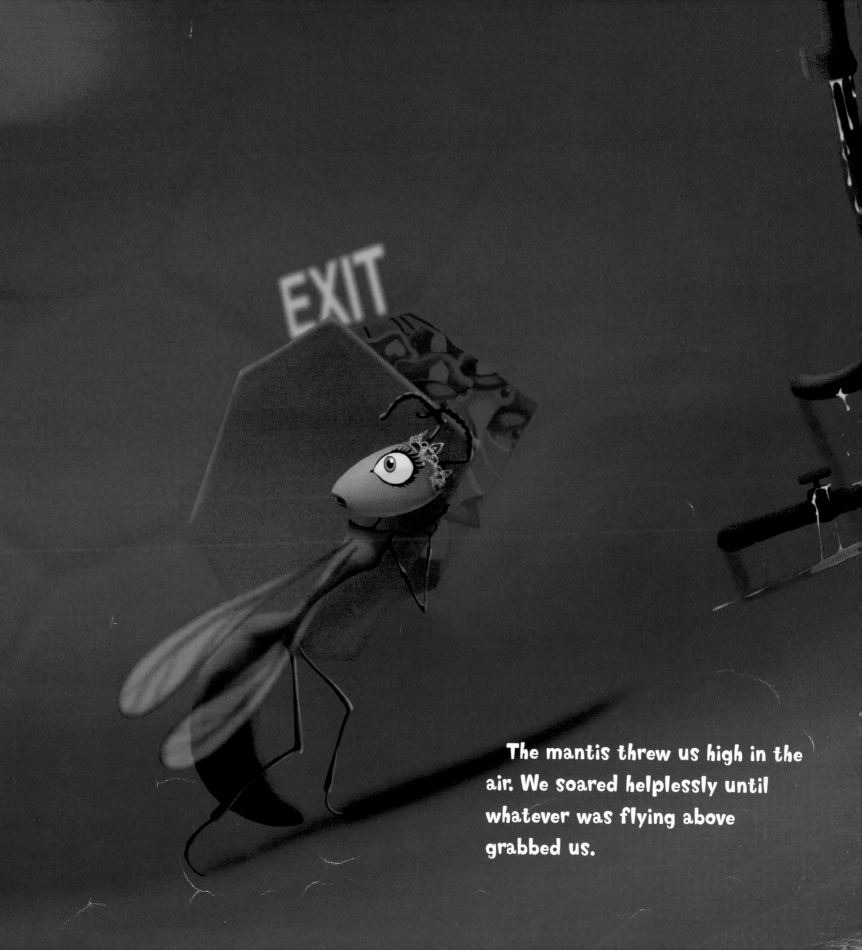

The mantis threw us high in the air. We soared helplessly until whatever was flying above grabbed us.

"Are we still on for those aphids, Acie?"
It wasn't a bat. It was Xerces. She had
rounded up every cop from here to
Termite Heights and brought
them to the HoneyWorks,
saving my wings again.

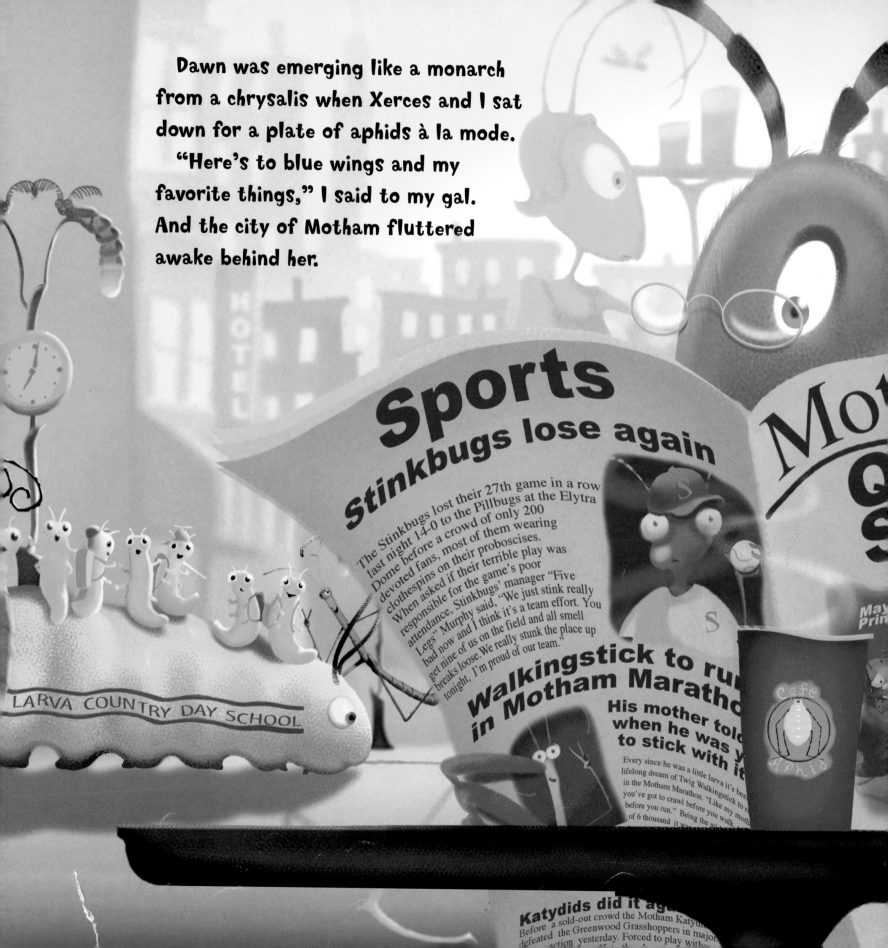

Dawn was emerging like a monarch from a chrysalis when Xerces and I sat down for a plate of aphids à la mode. "Here's to blue wings and my favorite things," I said to my gal. And the city of Motham fluttered awake behind her.

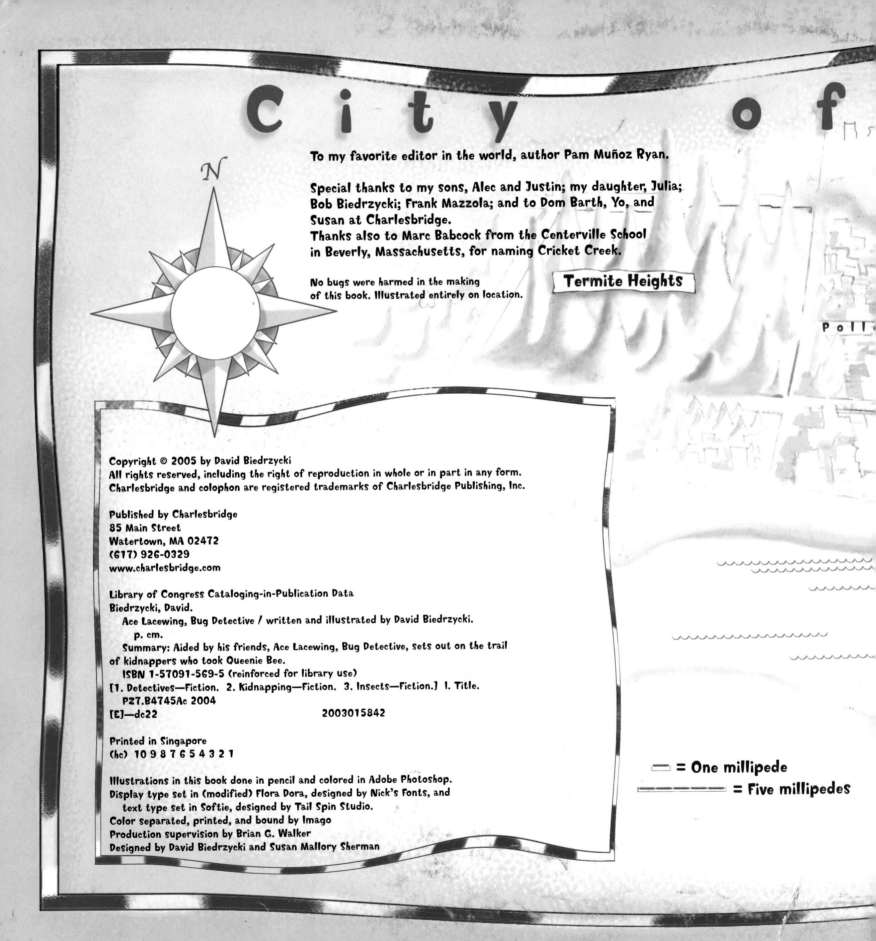

To my favorite editor in the world, author Pam Muñoz Ryan.

Special thanks to my sons, Alec and Justin; my daughter, Julia;
Bob Biedrzycki; Frank Mazzola; and to Dom Barth, Yo, and
Susan at Charlesbridge.
Thanks also to Marc Babcock from the Centerville School
in Beverly, Massachusetts, for naming Cricket Creek.

No bugs were harmed in the making
of this book. Illustrated entirely on location.

Termite Heights

Poll

Published by Charlesbridge
85 Main Street
Watertown, MA 02472
(617) 926-0329
www.charlesbridge.com

Library of Congress Cataloging-in-Publication Data
Biedrzycki, David.
    Ace Lacewing, Bug Detective / written and illustrated by David Biedrzycki.
      p. cm.
    Summary: Aided by his friends, Ace Lacewing, Bug Detective, sets out on the trail
of kidnappers who took Queenie Bee.
    ISBN 1-57091-569-5 (reinforced for library use)
[1. Detectives—Fiction. 2. Kidnapping—Fiction. 3. Insects—Fiction.] I. Title.
    PZ7.B4745Ac 2004
[E]—dc22   2003015842

Printed in Singapore
(hc) 10 9 8 7 6 5 4 3 2 1

Illustrations in this book done in pencil and colored in Adobe Photoshop.
Display type set in (modified) Flora Dora, designed by Nick's Fonts, and
    text type set in Softie, designed by Tail Spin Studio.
Color separated, printed, and bound by Imago
Production supervision by Brian G. Walker
Designed by David Biedrzycki and Susan Mallory Sherman

= One millipede
= Five millipedes